RAJA RAJA

ABOUT A THOUSAND YEARS AGO, PARANTAKA CHOLA II RULED OVER TANJAVUR IN SOUTH INDIA. HE HAD THREE CHILDREN, ADITYA KARIKALAN, ARUL MOZHI VERMAN AND KUNDAVAI.

BOTH KARIKALAN AND KUNDAVAI LOVED THEIR YOUNGER BROTHER.

AH! THERE HE COMES! HOW WELL HE RIDES!

YOU'RE LATE, ARUL. FATHER HAS SENT FOR ME. I'LL HAVE TO GO NOW.

I'LL COME WITH YOU.

1

YUVARAJA*KARIKALAN WAS AN AGGRESSIVE AND ARROGANT YOUTH. HE WAS UNPOPULAR AND HAD MANY ENEMIES.

THE WORST OF THEM WAS THE COMMANDER OF PARANTAKA'S ARMY. HE GLARED AT KARIKALAN AS HE STOOD BEFORE THE KING.

DID YOU WANT ME, FATHER?

YES, MY SON.

OUR COUNSELLORS SAY THAT VIRA PANDYA OF MADURAI HAS GROWN TROUBLESOME. CAN YOU TEACH HIM A LESSON, KARIKALAN?

WILLINGLY, FATHER. I SHALL MAKE YOU PROUD OF ME!

WHAT ABOUT ME, FATHER? MAY I ACCOMPANY HIM?

CERTAINLY! THAT'S WHAT I HAD HOPED TO HEAR YOU SAY.

* CROWN PRINCE

WHEN DO WE GO?

YOU MAY LEAVE AT ONCE. BUT I WOULD FIRST LIKE TO HAVE A FEW WORDS WITH YOU IN PRIVATE.

AS *THE COMMANDER TOOK THE HINT AND LEFT THE CHAMBER—*

MY SONS, MY HEART IS HEAVY.

WHY, DEAR FATHER? LET US SHARE YOUR BURDEN.

THE THRONE RIGHTFULLY BELONGS TO MY COUSIN, UTTAMA CHOLA.

WH-WHAT DO YOU MEAN, FATHER? I DON'T UNDERSTAND!

YEARS AGO UTTAMA'S SAINTLY FATHER GAVE IT UP TO HIS BROTHER, MY FATHER. UTTAMA, NOW WANTS IT BACK.

BUT I HAVE BEEN PRO-CLAIMED THE YUVARAJA! THIS COMES AS A SHOCK TO ME. WHAT SHALL I DO?

ARUL ANSWERED HIS QUERY.

OBEY FATHER'S WISHES.

PARANTAKA COULD NOT BEAR TO SEE KARIKALAN'S CRESTFALLEN FACE.

ALAS, MY SON, I AM SORRY. BUT MY CONSCIENCE TELLS ME I MUST RETURN IT. BESIDES···

···HE HAS MANY STRONG SUPPORTERS— AMONG THEM THE COMMANDER OF OUR ARMY AND HIS WIFE, NANDINI. AND THEY HATE YOU.

PLEASE GIVE ME LEAVE TO GO AWAY AND THINK OVER WHAT YOU'VE SAID, FATHER.

FOLLOWED BY ARUL, KARIKALAN WENT TO KUNDAVAI, AND UNBURDENED HIS HEART.

···THIS MEANS THAT I SHALL NOT SUCCEED FATHER.

DO NOT FRET, DEAR BROTHER.

WHEN YOU COME BACK VICTORIOUS FROM BATTLE, THE PEOPLE WILL CLAMOUR FOR YOU. THE COWARD UTTAMA WILL NOT STAND A CHANCE.

AT THAT MOMENT, VANDIYA DEVAN, A CLOSE FRIEND OF KARIKALAN, WALKED IN.

AH! THEN THERE IS SOME TRUTH IN THE RUMOURS I'VE HEARD. WHAT DO YOU PROPOSE TO DO?

KUNDAVAI HAD NO DOUBTS.

HE WILL FIGHT FOR WHAT IS HIS!

NO, BROTHER. YOU MUST DO YOUR DUTY. OBEY THE WISHES OF THE KING, OUR FATHER.

ARUL IS RIGHT, KARIKALAN. YOUR FATHER IS STILL THE KING.

WE GO OFF TO WAR TOMORROW. KUNDAVAI WILL BE LONELY. TAKE CARE OF HER.

I WILL. MAY YOU RETURN VICTORIOUS.

THE NEXT DAY, KARIKALAN AND ARUL RODE OUT TO MADURAI WITH THEIR FORCES.

THE TWO ARMIES MET—THE MIGHTY CHOLAS AND THE VALIANT PANDYAS.

THE BATTLE RAGED THROUGH THE DAY.

KARIKALAN AND ARUL FOUGHT FEARLESSLY. BUT VIRA PANDYA AND HIS MEN PUT UP A STOUT RESISTANCE.

ARUL WAS WORRIED.

OUR MEN ARE BRAVE BUT WE ARE OUTNUMBERED. O GOD, LET US NOT SUFFER DEFEAT.

TOWARDS SUNSET, HOWEVER, THE CHOLA ARMY GOT THE UPPER HAND AND DECIMATED THE PANDYA FORCES. VIRA PANDYA LOST HOPE.

THERE'S NO POINT IN CONTINUING THE BATTLE. I'D BETTER ESCAPE.

KARIKALAN, HOWEVER, SAW HIM FLEE.

NO, VIRA PANDYA! NOT A SINGLE PANDYA DESERVES TO LIVE. CERTAINLY NOT YOU— THEIR COWARDLY KING.

AND WITHOUT CONSULTING ARUL, KARIKALAN PURSUED THE RETREATING KING OF THE PANDYAS.

ISN'T THAT KARIKALAN? WHERE IS HE RIDING SO HARD?

HE HAS GONE AFTER VIRA PANDYA, SWEARING TO KILL HIM.

ARUL WAS DISMAYED.

MY BROTHER CAN BE RUTHLESS. I'D BETTER FOLLOW HIM.

MEANWHILE —

I AM BEING FOLLOWED! IT'S KARIKALAN, THE CHOLA PRINCE!

VIRA PANDYA SPURRED HIS HORSE ON. KARIKALAN MADE A QUICK DECISION.

HE KNOWS HE'S BEING FOLLOWED. I'LL RIDE OUT THROUGH THE TREES AND SURPRISE HIM FROM THE OPPOSITE DIRECTION.

BELIEVING THAT KARIKALAN HAD GIVEN UP THE CHASE, VIRA PANDYA SLACKENED HIS PACE. A LITTLE LATER—

AH! I'LL DISMOUNT AND REST HERE FOR A WHILE.

HE TETHERED HIS HORSE ...

...ENTERED THE DILAPIDATED HOUSE AND LAY DOWN TO REST.

A FEW MINUTES LATER, KARIKALAN RODE UP AND DISMOUNTED.

HIS HORSE! THE WEAKLING IS INSIDE.

DRAWING HIS SWORD...

...KARIKALAN CHARGED INTO THE HOUSE.

POOH! THE GREAT VIRA PANDYA EXHAUSTED SO SOON! GET UP YOU SCOUNDREL!

SPARE ME, KARIKALAN.

BUT KARIKALAN RAISED HIS SWORD AND—

A-AH!

BY THEN ARUL REACHED THE SCENE.

ALAS! I AM TOO LATE. WHAT HAVE YOU DONE!

10

LEAVE ME ALONE. I DID WHAT I HAD TO DO.

IT WAS NEITHER CHIVALROUS NOR WISE OF YOU.

ARUL WAS RIGHT. AT CAMP, NEXT DAY—

BEYOND DOUBT HE IS A GOOD WARRIOR. BUT THAT WAS A CRUEL THING TO DO— THE KING WAS RE-TREATING.

ARUL WOULD NEVER HAVE DONE THIS!

KARIKALAN HAD TO FACE THE HOSTILITY AND CONTEMPT OF HIS OWN SOLDIERS.

WHEN THE TRIUMPHANT BROTHERS RETURNED HOME, ARUL DISCUSSED THE VICTORY AND KARIKALAN'S DEED WITH KUNDAVAI AND VANDIYA DEVAN.

I WISH HE HAD SHOWN MORE RESTRAINT. HE HAS ANTAGONISED THE COMMANDER OF OUR ARMY.

WHY?

DON'T YOU KNOW? THE COMMANDER'S WIFE, NANDINI, HAD BEEN BROUGHT UP BY VIRA PANDYA.

NOW EVEN KARIKALAN'S FRIENDS ARE DESERTING HIM ONE BY ONE.

NOT ME.

YOU HAVE ALWAYS BEEN LOYAL TO US.

IF ONLY YOU KNEW WHY! DEAR, DEAR KUNDAVAI!

JUST THEN, A COURT ATTENDANT ENTERED THE ROOM.

ARUL, THE KING WISHES TO SEE YOU.

PERHAPS HE INTENDS SENDING YOU TO LANKA.* SO I HEARD.

ARUL WAS DELIGHTED.

THEN I MUST GO TO HIM AT ONCE.

AS ARUL STOOD EXPECTANTLY BEFORE HIS FATHER —

ARUL, MY SON, YOU HAVE ALWAYS SHOWN GREATER RESTRAINT THAN YOUR BROTHER. SO I HAVE DECIDED TO SEND YOU ON AN ASSIGNMENT.

WHERE TO, FATHER?

TO LANKA. KING MAHENDRA HAS RISEN IN RE-BELLION. GO AND QUELL HIM.

I CANNOT WAIT TO LEAVE, FATHER. I AM EAGER FOR VICTORY!

*THE ISLAND OF CEYLON NOW KNOWN AS SRI LANKA.

BEFORE DEPARTING, ARUL WENT TO TAKE LEAVE OF HIS BELOVED, THE PRINCESS VANATI.

DON'T WEEP, VANATI.

MUST YOU GO SO SOON?

VANATI'S FATHER, VIKRAMA KESI, OVERHEARD THEM.

FOR SHAME, VANATI. A NOBLE PRINCE'S DUTY IS TO FIGHT. WHAT IS MORE, ARUL IS DESTINED TO BE KING ONE DAY.

HAVE YOU FORGOTTEN UNCLE UTTAMA AND MY ELDER BROTHER?

I HAVEN'T. BUT WE ARE IN NEED OF A BRAVE, NOBLE KING. MAY ALL SUCCESS BE YOURS.

GOD BE WITH YOU.

THE NEXT DAY, ARUL AND HIS MEN SET SAIL FOR LANKA.

AT LANKA —

TOMORROW WE ATTACK. LET US GET ALL THE REST WE CAN TONIGHT. GOOD-NIGHT, MY MEN.

BEFORE DAWN THE CHOLA ARMY ADVANCED UPON ITS UNSUSPECTING FOES···

...AND OVERPOWERED THEM. MAHENDRA DECIDED TO FLEE.

WHAT A DEFEAT! I MUST ESCAPE TO THE HILLS BEFORE IT'S TOO LATE.

MAHENDRA WAS AT ARUL'S MERCY.

SHALL I STOP HIM AND FINISH HIM OFF, SIR? IT SHOULD BE EASY.

NO. LET HIM GO.

ARUL'S GENEROUS ACT MADE HIS SOLDIERS ADMIRE HIM EVEN MORE.

WHAT WE NEED IS A KING OF HIS STATURE. BRAVE AND STRONG YET COURTEOUS, KIND AND CHIVALROUS. HE BREATHES NOBILITY.

MEANWHILE, AT TANJAVUR, UTTAMA WAS CLOSETED WITH THE COMMANDER OF THE CHOLA ARMY AND HIS WIFE, NANDINI.

THAT COWARD KARIKALAN HAS EARNED THE ADMIRATION OF THE KING...

BUT ONLY THE CONTEMPT OF THE PEOPLE. THEY HATE HIM FOR HIS UNCHIVALROUS ACT.

AH, DEAR HUSBAND, THEN AVENGE THE DEATH OF VIRA PANDYA, WHO BROUGHT ME UP, KILL KARIKALAN.

AND MAKE THE WAY CLEAR FOR ARUL? THE PEOPLE LOVE HIM AND HE IS THE SON OF THE KING!

NO, IF YOU KILL KARIKALAN, ARUL WILL BE FRIGHTENED AWAY.

SHE'S RIGHT. I MUST MAKE SURE A PRINCE I CAN COMMAND IS CROWNED KING — SOMEONE LIKE UTTAMA.

AND I'LL GET THE THRONE.

THE COMMANDER DID NOT WASTE ANY TIME.

PLEASE MEET ME, ALONE, TONIGHT AT THE OLD RUINS.

THE COMMANDER THEN TURNED TO A RUFFIAN IN HIS PAY.

THE MEN WILL BE WAITING FOR HIM AT THE RUINS...

YES, SIR. DO NOT WORRY. IT WILL ALL WORK AS PLANNED. I MUST LEAVE NOW.

WHEN KARIKALAN RECEIVED THE NOTE —

I WONDER WHY VANDIYA DEVAN HAS ASKED ME TO MEET HIM THERE. STRANGE! BUT I'D BETTER GO.

THAT NIGHT, AS KARIKALAN WAITED AT THE RUINS—

THERE HE IS! SHALL I KILL HIM?

LET US DO IT TO-GETHER, BUT QUICK-LY AND QUIETLY.

THOUGH THEY HAD SPOKEN IN WHISPERS, KARIKALAN'S EARS WERE SHARP.

WHO ARE YOU? WHY ARE YOU HERE?

TO AVENGE THE PANDYAS. DIE, SCOUNDREL.

A-A-AH

IT WAS DAWN WHEN THE RUTHLESS KILLERS RODE BACK TO THE CITY.

HAVE YOU HEARD THE NEWS? THE YUVARAJA HAS BEEN MURDERED.

MURDERED! THE KING WILL HAVE TO RECALL ARUL FROM LANKA.

THE NEWS SOON REACHED THE PALACE.

OH PRINCESS, THE YUVARAJA HAS BEEN MURDERED! NEAR THE RUINS!

KUNDAVAI WAS SHOCKED.

NO! IT CANNOT BE TRUE. IT'S A LIE.

CALM YOURSELF, DEAR PRINCESS. I WILL GO AND FIND OUT IF WHAT HE SAYS IS TRUE.

VANDIYA DEVAN RODE OUT TO THE RUINS.

AH! MY DEAR FRIEND! WHO COULD HAVE DONE THIS FOUL DEED! I MUST GO TO THE KING.

PARANTAKA ALMOST BROKE DOWN WHEN VANDIYA DEVAN GAVE HIM THE NEWS.

ALAS! MY DEAR KARIKALAN GONE! WHAT IS THERE LEFT FOR ME?

THEN, CONTROLING HIMSELF HE LOOKED UP.

GO, VANDIYA DEVAN. BRING ARUL BACK AT ONCE.

I MUST HAVE UTTAMA CROWNED BEFORE ARUL RETURNS.

A FEW DAYS LATER, AT LANKA A PALACE ATTENDANT STOOD BEFORE ARUL.

YOUR EXCELLENCY, A MESSENGER FROM YOUR FATHER AWAITS YOUR PLEASURE.

SHOW HIM IN.

WHEN THE MESSENGER WALKED IN—

VANDIYA DEVAN! WHAT BRINGS YOU HERE? COME SIT DOWN.

I BRING BAD NEWS. KARIKALAN HAS BEEN MURDERED. YOUR FATHER NEEDS YOU.

ARUL BORE THE NEWS BRAVELY AND CALMLY.

LET US LEAVE IMMEDIATELY.

BUT SIR— THE WEATHER...

MY FATHER NEEDS ME. I MUST GO TO HIM IMMEDIATELY.

SO, DESPITE THE BREWING STORM, ARUL AND VANDIYA DEVAN SET SAIL.

BUT THE SHIP NEVER REACHED SHORE.

ARUL AND VANDIYA DEVAN, HOWEVER, SURVIVED AND TOOK SHELTER WITH SOME BUDDHIST MONKS AT NAGAPATTINAM.

MEANWHILE AT TANJAVUR, THE COMMANDER PRESSED THE AILING KING TO INSTALL UTTAMA AS THE CROWN PRINCE.

DO NOT DELAY ANY MORE, SIR. IT IS NOT WISE.

YES, YES! I KNOW. BUT LET ARUL RETURN.

AT THAT MOMENT ARUL AND VANDIYA DEVAN WALKED IN.

DO MY EYES DECEIVE ME? IS THAT YOU ARUL?

YES, FATHER. I HAVE COME.

AND RUINED MY PLANS.

ARUL, MY DAYS ARE NUMBERED. WHAT SHOULD I DO? YOUR BROTHER IS DEAD. WE HAVE NO YUVARAJA AND... AND...

ARUL UNDERSTOOD WHAT HIS FATHER FOUND DIFFICULT TO UTTER.

FATHER I SHALL MAKE ARRANGEMENTS FOR UTTAMA TO BE INSTALLED AS YUVARAJA.

PARANTAKA WAS RELIEVED.

I KNEW I COULD COUNT ON YOU, MY NOBLE, DUTIFUL SON.

ARUL AND VANDIYA DEVAN LEFT PARANTAKA AND WENT TO SEE UTTAMA.

ARUL! VANDIYA DEVAN! YOU ARE BACK! B-BUT... I THOUGHT... I HEARD...

WHAT YOU HEARD WAS TRUE. OUR SHIP SANK. BUT WE SURVIVED.

IN THE INTERESTS OF OUR KINGDOM LET US QUARREL NO MORE, UNCLE. IT IS MY FATHER'S WILL AND MINE THAT YOU BE INSTALLED AS THE YUVARAJA.

PROVE YOURSELF WORTHY AND RULE WISELY.

UTTAMA COULD NOT BELIEVE HIS EARS.

BUT...DON'T YOU WANT TO BE KING?

I DID ONCE HOPE TO SUCCEED MY BROTHER. BUT NOT AFTER I LEARNED THAT THE RIGHT TO THE THRONE WAS YOURS.

WHAT A NOBLE SOUL! HE HAS MY RESPECT AND ADMIRATION.

NOT LONG AFTER, PARANTAKA DIED.

DO NOT WEEP, SISTER. WE HAVE WORK AHEAD OF US. I HAVE TO PLACE UTTAMA ON THE THRONE.

AND ARRANGE FOR YOUR MARRIAGE TO ME, KUNDAVAI.

UTTAMA'S CORONATION SOON TOOK PLACE.

THE KING SHALL HAVE OUR LOYALTY. ARUL SUPPORTS HIM.

LONG LIVE ARUL MOZHI VARMAN!

A FEW WEEKS LATER, ARUL AND VANDIYA DEVAN WERE TOGETHER IN KUNDAVAI'S ROOM.

HOW MUCH MY LEARNED SISTER AND YOU HAVE IN COMMON, VANDIYA DEVAN!

THEN WHY DON'T YOU UNITE US FOR EVER IN MARRIAGE?

ARUL WAS PLEASANTLY SURPRISED. HE HAD NEVER SUSPECTED THAT HIS FRIEND LOVED HIS SISTER.

WITH PLEASURE, VANDIYA DEVAN, IF KUNDAVAI IS WILLING.

CAUGHT OFF HER GUARD, KUNDAVAI COULD ONLY TURN AWAY BASHFULLY.

AS ARUL WALKED OUT OF THE ROOM—

I, TOO, MUST NOT KEEP VANATI WAITING ANY LONGER.

HE WENT TO VIKRAMA KESI.

UNCLE, THE PERIOD OF MOURNING FOR MY FATHER IS OVER. VANATI AND I HAVE WAITED LONG.

MY SON, I HAVE BEEN WAITING FOR THIS DAY. LET THE WEDDING TAKE PLACE AS SOON AS POSSIBLE.

THE WEDDING OF ARUL TO VANATI AND KUNDAVAI TO VANDIYA DEVAN WERE PERFORMED ON THE SAME DAY.

AND IN TIME, A SON RAJENDRA AND A DAUGHTER KUNDAVI WERE BORN TO ARUL AND VANATI.

TWELVE YEARS HAD GONE BY. UTTAMA CHOLA WAS ON HIS DEATH-BED.

SIR, THE KING IS VERY ILL AND WISHES TO SEE YOU.

I SHALL COME AT ONCE.

ARUL HURRIED TO HIS UNCLE'S BEDSIDE.

I AM DYING AND HAVE NO STRENGTH. I WANT TO TELL YOU THAT I AM INDEBTED TO YOU. YOU WILL MAKE A BETTER KING THAN I HAVE BEEN.

HUSH, UNCLE. YOU MUST NOT TIRE YOURSELF.

SOON AFTER, UTTAMA CHOLA DIED. ARUL MOZHI VARMAN WAS CROWNED RAJA RAJA CHOLA AND KUNDAVAI, CO-RULER.

ONE DAY VANDIYA DEVAN CAME TO HIM.

OUR SPIES TELL US THAT THE WEAK KING OF MADURAI IS ONCE AGAIN IN ARMS AGAINST US, THIS TIME IN LEAGUE WITH THE CHERA KING.

27

THE FORT WAS SOON TAKEN.

VICTORY TO RAJA RAJA CHOLA!

THE GATES ARE OPEN!

LATER —

VANDIYA DEVAN, SINCE BOTH KINGS HAVE SURRENDERED, LET US RETURN HOME.

BACK IN TANJAVUR —

BROTHER, OUR REIGN HAS STARTED WELL!

BUT WE HAVE NEWS THAT THE KING OF LANKA IS UP IN ARMS AGAIN. WE WILL HAVE TO LEAVE FOR LANKA.

AS THEY DISCUSSED THE STRATEGY THEY SHOULD ADOPT—

OUR SHIPS ARE STURDY AND OUR SAILORS BRAVE. PERHAPS...

DO YOU PLAN TO FIGHT THEM AT SEA?

WE WILL FIGHT THEM BOTH AT SEA AND ON LAND! LET ALL KINGS FEAR OUR NAVY AS THEY DO OUR ARMY.

THE CHOLA SHIPS SET OFF ON THEIR FIRST NAVAL EXPEDITION.

IN A SHORT TIME, ALL THE MAJOR FORTS WERE SEIZED.

THEN, MARCHING INTO THE COUNTRY, THEY SOON CAPTURED MANY VILLAGES AND TOWNS.

WE HAVE DRIVEN THEIR KING AWAY AND TAKEN THEIR TOWNS. FROM NOW ON THIS PROVINCE IS OURS.

LET US SET UP A NEW CAPITAL HERE.

WHAT FURTHER CONQUESTS ARE YOU PLANNING NOW, BROTHER?

MUST HE FOREVER BE PLANNING CONQUESTS?

AH, VANATI. IF I DID NOT WAGE WAR WHERE WOULD OUR KINGDOM BE?

AS THE YEARS ROLLED ON RAJA RAJA CHOLA'S PRESTIGE AS A POWERFUL BUT JUST RULER GREW. HIS ENEMIES HE QUELLED. THOSE WHO SOUGHT ASYLUM WITH HIM DID NOT DO SO IN VAIN. SUCH WAS THE REIGN OF RAJA RAJA CHOLA THE GREAT.

Amar Chitra Katha's

EXCITING STORY CATEGORIES, ONE AMAZING DESTINATION.

From the episodes of Mahabharata to the wit of Birbal,
from the valour of Shivaji to the teachings of Tagore,
from the adventures of Pratapan to the tales of Ruskin Bond –
Amar Chitra Katha stories span across different genres to get you the best of literature.